J
E

Osborne, Mary Pope

Moonhorse

DUE DATE

			(4-8)

Moonhorse

by Mary Pope Osborne
illustrated by
S. M. Saelig

Alfred A. Knopf · New York

This is a Borzoi Book published by Alfred A. Knopf, Inc.

Text copyright © 1991 by Mary Pope Osborne
Illustrations copyright © 1991 by S. M. Saelig
All rights reserved under International and Pan-American
Copyright Conventions. Published in the United States by
Alfred A. Knopf, Inc., New York, and simultaneously in
Canada by Random House of Canada Limited, Toronto.
Distributed by Random House, Inc., New York.

Book design by Mina Greenstein
Manufactured in the United States of America
10   9   8   7   6   5   4   3   2   1

Library of Congress Cataloging-in-Publication Data
Osborne, Mary Pope. Moonhorse.
Summary: A winged horse takes a child on a wonderful
night journey into outer space.   [1. Outer space—Fiction.
2. Horses—Fiction]   I. S. M. Saelig, ill.   II. Title.
PZ7.081167MP   1991   [E]   87-3818
ISBN 0-394-88960-6   ISBN 0-394-98960-0 (lib. bdg.)

To the memory of my father
M. P. O.

To Dorothy
S. M. S.

We rock on the porch,
my dad and I,
while a thin moon hides
behind the trees.

In the distance a whistle blows.
A flock of blackbirds
leaves the grass.

Then I see a star, first star tonight.
"Look, Dad," I say, "let's make a wish!"
But Daddy's quiet;
he's gone to sleep.

Now I feel lonely in the dark.
So I make a wish
by myself.

The wind starts to blow,
and birds start to cry.

Out of the night
the Moonhorse appears.

I slip from Dad's lap
and run through the grass.
I touch the white horse
and whisper, "Hey, boy."
He nuzzles my cheek.

I grab his white mane
and climb on his back,

and we rise
through the night.

We fly over mountains,
through cloud-stuff and mist,

high over twilight,

till we land on a star.

I water the Moonhorse,
brush dust from his eyes.
Together we lasso
the new moon below.

We pull very hard.
Then the Moonhorse and I
pull the Moon through the sky!

We ride by the Dipper
and wave to the Bear,

yell to the Goat,
"Watch out! Moon coming by!"

The Scorpion rises,
but we're not afraid—

Archer stands guard
with a bow made of stars.

Wolf shadows chase us!
"Fly, Moonhorse, fly!"

Then a comet shoots past,
and we leap, lose the wolves
in a shower of light.

We gallop toward midnight,
the Moonhorse and I,
pulling the Moon
through the clear silent sky,

past red stars and blue stars,

the Herdsman,

the Ram.

Breathless, we climb
to the top
of the night.

Then I tell the new moon,
"We have to go now.
You can drift on your own
down to the dawn.
You're safe from the shadows
and the Scorpion, too."

The Moonhorse and I say
good night to our Moon,
let go of our rope
and sail back to earth.

We float through the darkness,
through stardust and clouds,

down through the sky,
till we land in our yard.

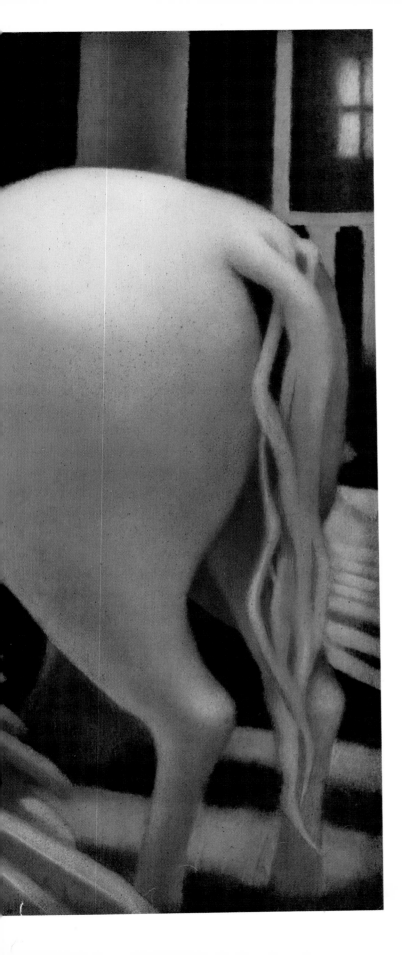

I hug the Moonhorse,
say gently,
"Sorry to go,
but my dad needs me now."

He stands by the trees
till I'm safe on the porch.

Daddy's still sleeping,
so I tap on his head
and whisper, "Wake up.
You rocked off to sleep."

"Goodness," he says,
"the Moon's high in the sky."
"I know it. We helped her."
"Who?"
"The Moonhorse and I."

Wind starts to blow,
and birds start to cry.

Swish, swish…
"What's that?" Daddy says.

"Wings, Dad.
Wave good-bye."